ALPHABET PRAYERS
FOR TODDLERS

WRITTEN BY: LINDSEY GRAHAM
ILLUSTRATED BY: MICHAEL R. VOOGD

Quantity sales and special discounts are available for bulk purchases by corporations, associations and others. For details, please reach out to CSI Publishing, listed above.

Orders by U.S. trade bookstores and wholesalers,
Email: ken@clientsi.com

The author can be reached through Ken Walls.

Manufactured and printed in the United States of America, distributed globally by CSI Publishing - www.csipublishing.com

Dallas, Texas

Library of Congress Control Number: 2024910512

ISBN: 978-1-963986-03-7 - Hardcover

ISBN: 978-1-963986-04-4 - Paperback

ISBN: 978-1-963986-05-1 - eBook

DEDICATION PAGE

I DEDICATE THIS BOOK TO ALL MY CHILDREN,
BORN AND UNBORN.

TRIGGER, OAKLEY AND RANGER,
BEAUTIFUL BABIES THAT GOD GAVE LIFE TO
ON EARTH.

BUT ALSO THE FOUR BABIES THAT WERE LOST IN MY
WOMB WHOSE LIVES MATTER JUST AS MUCH.

YOU ARE MY PURPOSE AND THE GREATEST JOY AND
ADVENTURE OF MY LIFE. LOVE, MOMMY

ISAIAH 54:13
ALL YOUR CHILDREN SHALL BE TAUGHT BY THE LORD,
AND GREAT SHALL BE THE PEACE OF YOUR CHILDREN.

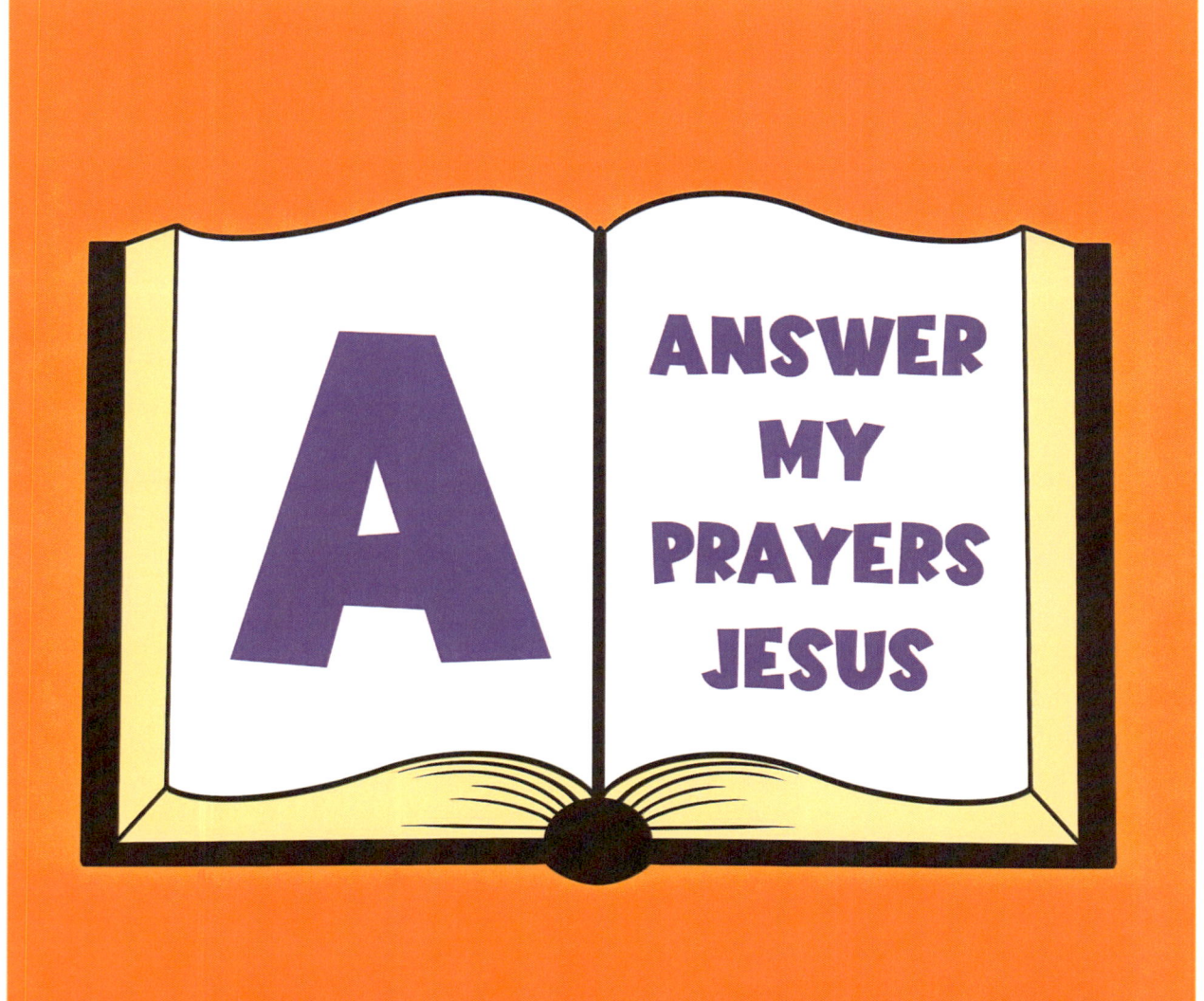

He answered their prayers because they trusted in Him.
1 Chronicles 5:20

If you fully obey the Lord your God and carefully follow all his commands I give you today, the Lord your God will set you high above all the nations on earth.
Deuteronomy 28:1

The Lord protects the simple hearted; when I was in great need, he saved me.
PSALM 116:6

As for God, His way is perfect; the word of the Lord is flawless.
2 Samuel 22:31

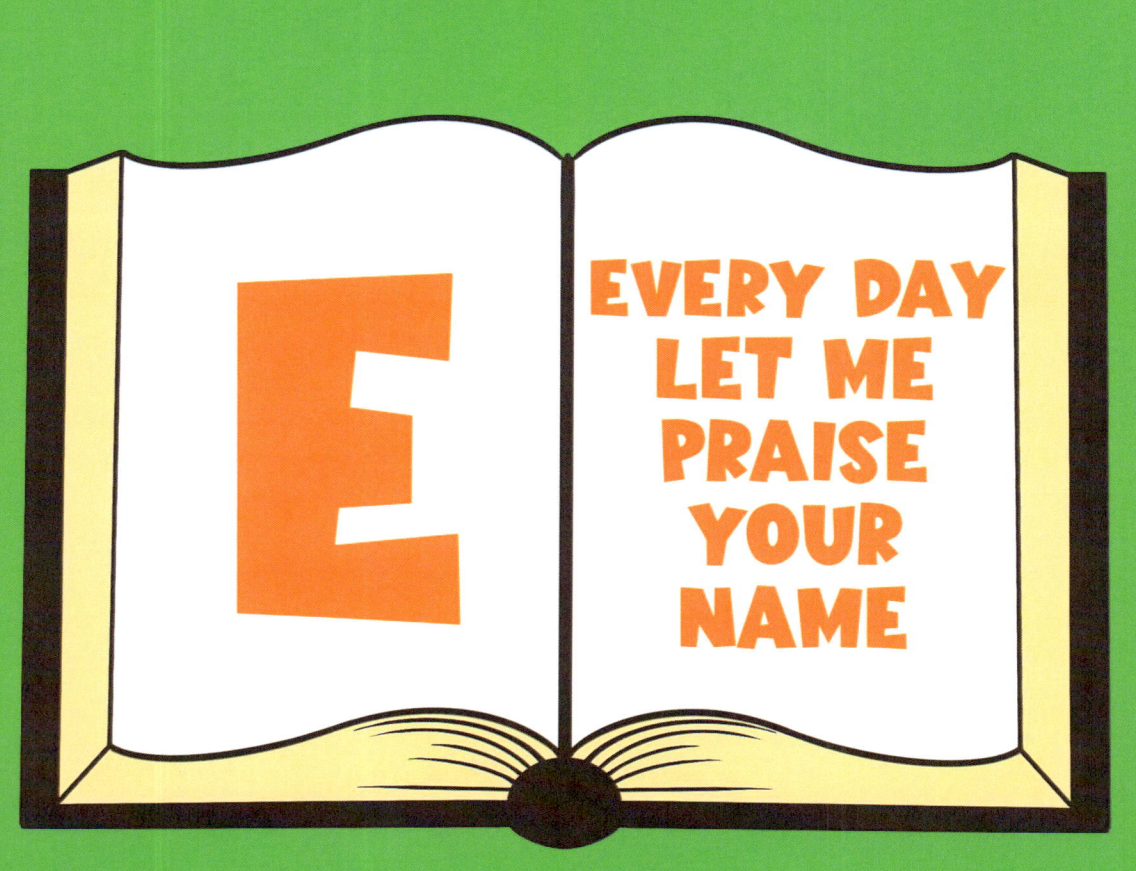

E EVERY DAY LET ME PRAISE YOUR NAME

Let everything that has breath
praise the Lord.
PSALM 150:6

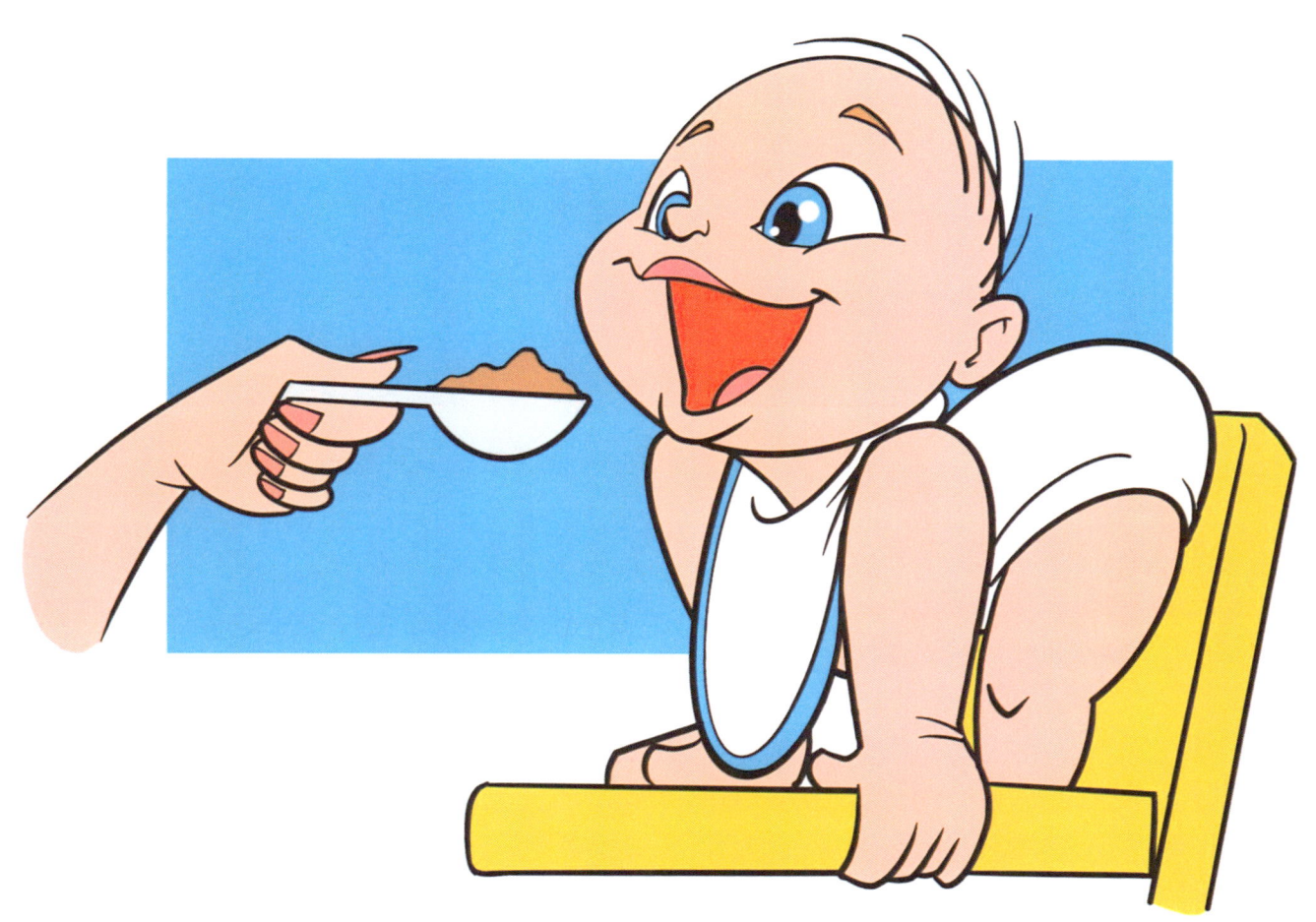

Show me your ways, O Lord, teach me your paths; guide me in your truth and teach me, for you are God my savior, and my hope is in you all day long.
PSALM 25:5

But God demonstrates his own love for us in this:while we were still sinners, Christ died for us.
Romans 5:8

HELP ME
TO BE
THANKFUL

Be joyful always; pray continually; give thanks in all circumstances, for this is God's will for you in Christ Jesus. 1 Thessalonians 5:16

MY SOUL YEARNS
FOR YOU IN THE
NIGHT; IN THE
MORNING MY SPIRIT
LONGS FOR YOU.
ISAIAH 26:9

But as for me and my house, we will serve the Lord.
Joshua 24:15

Do not fear, for I am with you; do not be dismayed, for I am your God. I will strengthen you and help you; I will uphold you with my righteous right hand.
Isaiah 41:10

Surely you desire truth in the inner parts; you teach me wisdom in the inmost place.
PSALM 51:6

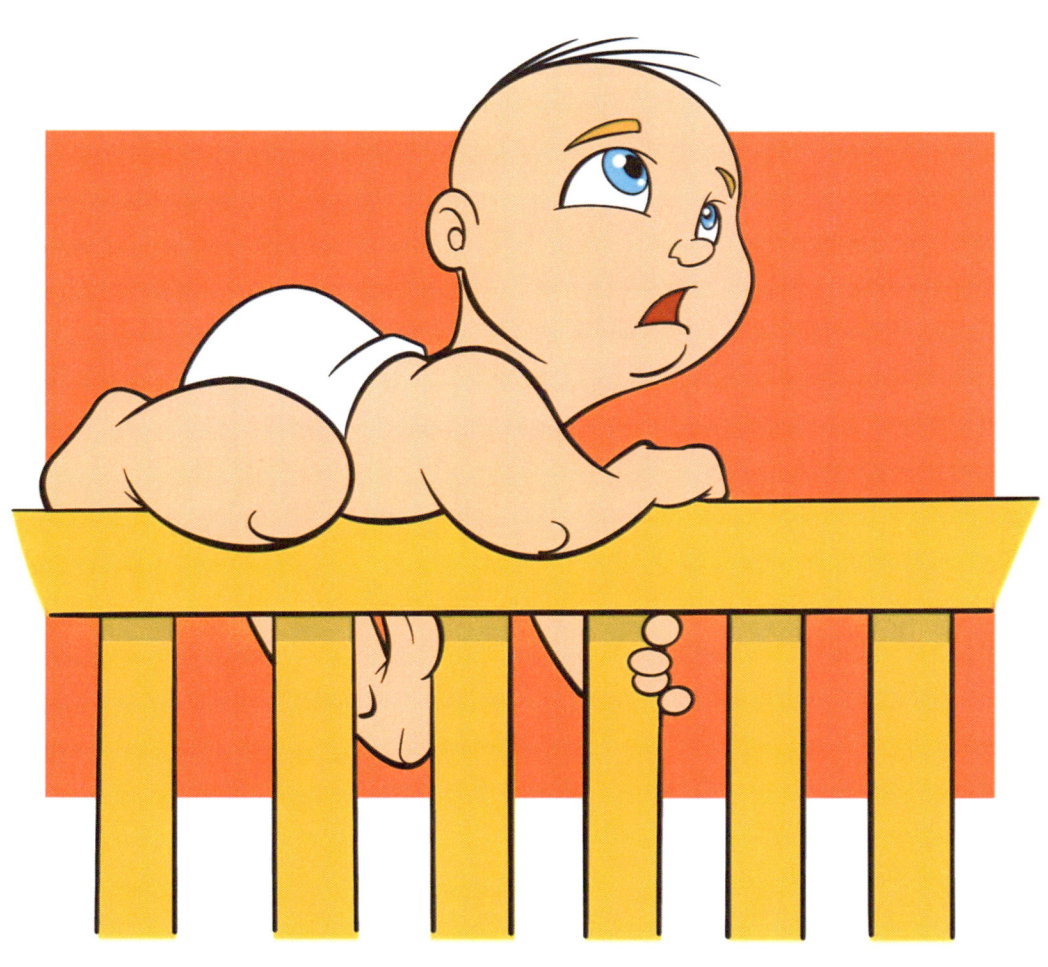

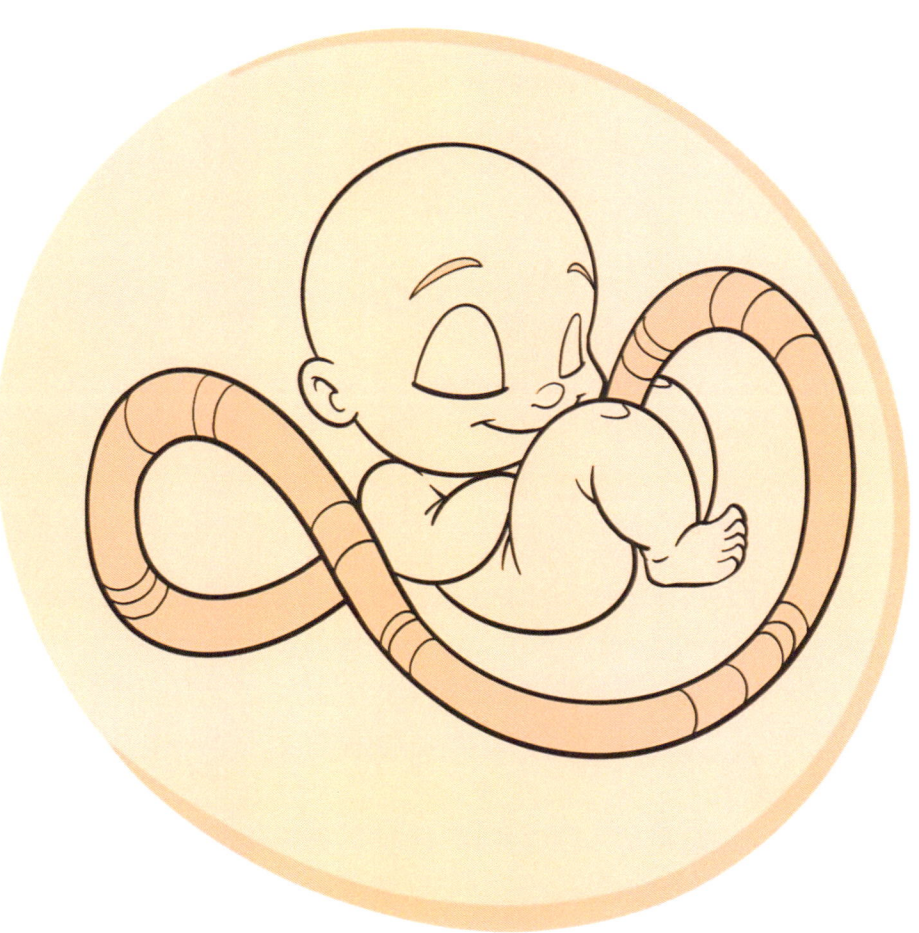

Therefore, if anyone is in Christ, he is a new creation; the old has gone, the new has come!
2 Corinthians 5:17

DO YOU NOT KNOW THAT YOU ARE THE
TEMPLE OF GOD AND THAT THE
HOLY SPIRIT DWELLS IN YOU.
I CORINTHIANS 3:16

create in me a pure heart, O God, and renew a steadfast spirit within me.
PSALM 51:10

P

PLACE
YOUR
PROTECTION
OVER ME

No one will ever be able to stand up against you all the days of your life. As I was with Moses, so I will be with you; I will never leave you nor forsake you.
Joshua 1:5

I have told you these things, so that in me you may have peace. In this world you will have trouble. But take heart! I have overcome the world.
John 16:33

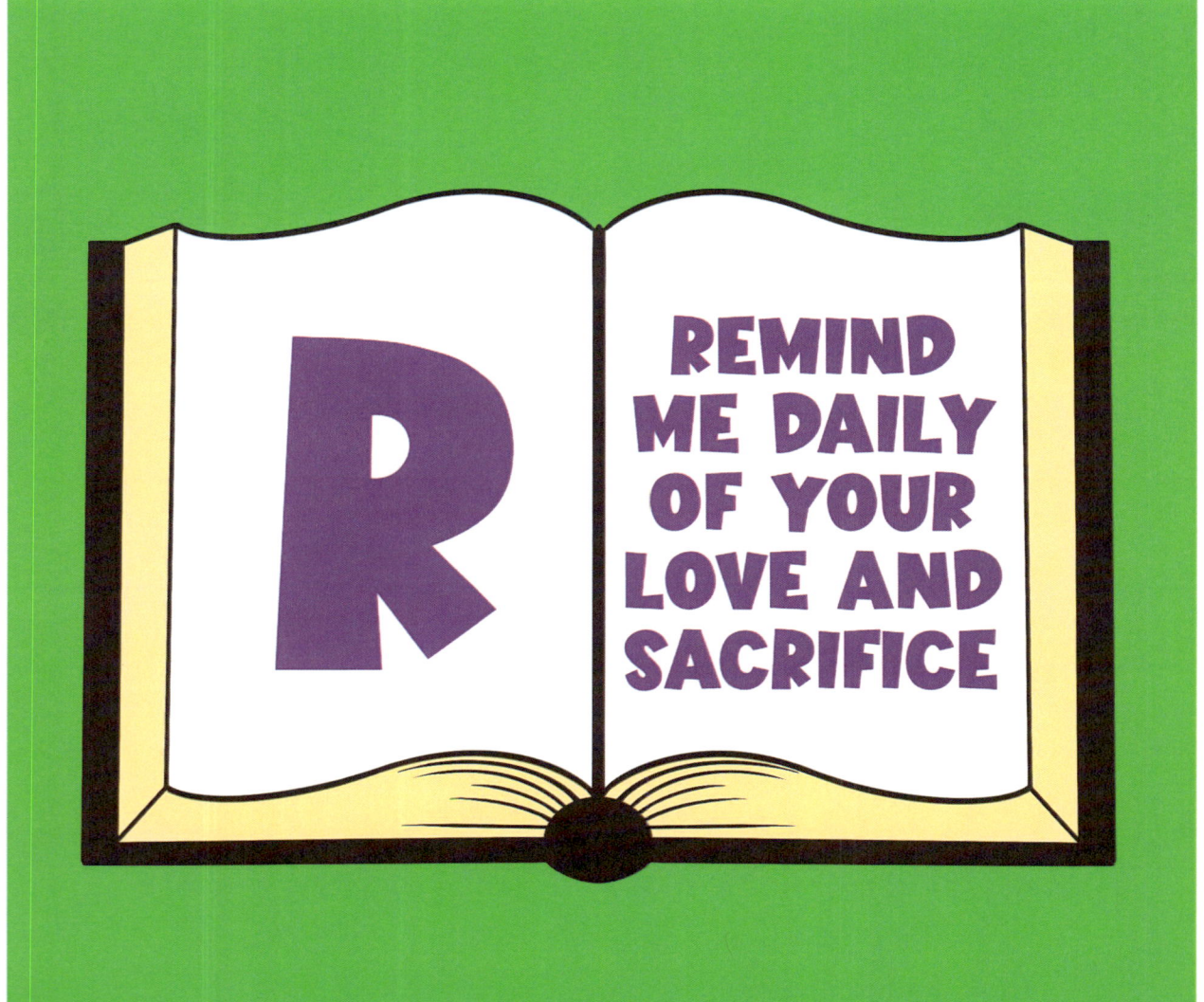

For God so loved the world that he gave his one and only son, that whoever believes in him shall not perish but have eternal life.
John 3:16

The Lord is close to the brokenhearted and saves those who are crushed in spirit.
A righteous man may have many troubles, but the Lord delivers him from them all.
PSALM 34:17-19

And we know that in all things God works for the good of those who love Him.
Romans 8:28

CALL to me and I will answer you
and tell you great and unsearchable
things you do not know.
Jeremiah 33:3

He has showed you, O man, what is good.
And what does the Lord require of you?
To act justly and to love mercy and to
walk humbly with your God.
Micah 6:8

If the Lord delights in a man's way, he makes his steps firm; though he stumble, he will not fall, for the Lord upholds him with his hand.
PSALM 37:23

Because he loves me, says the Lord, I will rescue him; I will protect him, for he acknowledges my name. He will call upon me and I will answer him.
PSALM 91:14-15

Trust in the Lord, with all your heart, and lean, not on your own understanding.

In all your ways, acknowledge him, and he shall direct your path.
Proverbs 3:5-6

SPECIAL THANKS:

VIVIANNA THOMAS

KRISTAN WHANN

JULIET COLLINS

JON FILBERT

SCOTT GRAHAM

SHERRIL WILSON

BLAKE REYNOLDS

PAMELA POWELL

**YOUR WORD IS A LAMP TO MY FEET
AND A LIGHT TO MY PATH
PSALM 119:105**

ABOUT THE AUTHOR
LINDSEY GRAHAM, THE PATRIOT BARBIE

MOST WIDELY KNOWN FOR DEFYING GOVERNMENT LOCKDOWNS IN 2020, LINDSEY WAS CATAPULTED INTO A GLOBAL SPOTLIGHT. SHE OPENED HER SALON AGAINST NATIONAL MANDATES, HAD HER LIVELIHOOD AND CHILDREN THREATENED AND BECAME THE ICONIC VOICE OF FREEDOM, BEING LABELED "THE PATRIOT BARBIE" BY THE WOKE MOB. LOSING 6 BUSINESSES, FLEEING HER HOME STATE AND CONTINUING TO FIGHT FOR HER FAMILY, LINDSEY STEPPED INTO A NEW CALLING.

GOD HAD A GREATER PURPOSE FOR THIS WIFE AND MOM OF THREE. HE CALLED LINDSEY INTO A LIFE OF ACTIVISM AND FREEDOM FIGHTING. LINDSEY HAS BECOME AN ENCOURAGING KEYNOTE SPEAKER, AUTHOR, NEWS PERSONALITY, POWERFUL PODCAST GUEST AND AN INFLUENTIAL LEADER ONLINE, BOLDLY GLORIFYING GOD IN HER JOURNEY.

AFTER HER VIRAL SPEECH AT A SCHOOL BOARD MEETING DRESSED AS A CAT IN 2022, HER FIGHT BOLDENED. SHE BECAME A LEADER AGAINST FEMINISM AND AN ADVOCATE FOR REAL WOMEN'S RIGHTS, THE NUCLEAR FAMILY, BUT MOST IMPORTANTLY, THE PROTECTION AND INNOCENCE OF OUR CHILDREN, LINDSEY HAS DIVINELY FOUND GOD'S PLACE FOR HER AND AND HER VOICE AT THE FRONT OF THE BATTLE LINES FOR WOMEN, PRE BORN BABIES AND MOMS.
SHE IS THE FIERCE, BOLD AND UNAPOLOGETIC VOICE FOR PATRIOTS ACROSS AMERICA.

LINDSEY IS A NATIONAL KEYNOTE SPEAKER AND THE AUTHOR OF THE BOOK TARGETED: ONE MOMS FIGHT FOR LIFE, LIBERTY AND THE PURSUIT OF HAPPINESS, HER MEMOIR. SHE IS THE CEO OF THE PATRIOT BARBIE SHOP AND A CO-FOUNDER OF A CHRISTIAN WOMEN'S FASHION BRAND, PRETTY LITTLE PATRIOT. SHE IS ALSO AN AMBASSADOR FOR TURNING POINT USA.
FIND HER COMPLETE STORY AND MOVEMENT ON PATRIOTBARBIE.COM

JESUS SAID, "LET THE LITTLE CHILDREN COME TO ME, AND DO NOT HINDER THEM, FOR THE KINGDOM OF HEAVEN BELONGS TO SUCH AS THESE." MATTHEW 19:14

TAKE YOUR TINY TOT ON A JOURNEY WITH JESUS EVERY EVENING (OR ANY TIME) AS YOU TEACH YOUR SWEET TODDLER HOW TO PRAY, WHAT TO PRAY FOR, AND TIE IT ALL TOGETHER WITH TRUE BIBLICAL TEACHING, INCLUDING SCRIPTURE REFERENCES.

YOUR CHILD WILL QUICKLY LEARN THEIR ALPHABET, BUT MORE IMPORTANTLY LEARN TO CORRELATE EACH LETTER WITH A BOLD PRAYER TO THEIR SAVIOR.

ALPHABET PRAYERS FOR TODDLERS WILL EXPAND YOUR CHILD'S READING CAPABILITIES, MEMORY, ALPHABET, SCRIPTURE KNOWLEDGE AND FAITH. EVEN MORE GLORIOUS, IS THE PRECIOUS TIME SPENT TOGETHER, TEACHING YOUR CHILD TO TALK TO JESUS. AS YOUR CHILD GROWS, HE OR SHE WILL HOPEFULLY BE ABLE TO READ THESE PRAYERS TO YOU BY MEMORY.